JOKER'S JOYRIDE

By D. R. Shealy

Illustrated by Erik Doescher, Mike DeCarlo, and David Tanguay

Random House 🏠 New York

DC SUPER FRIENDS and all related titles, characters, and elements are trademarks of DC Comics. Copyright © 2010 DC Comics. All rights reserved.
Published in the United States by Random House Children's Books, a division of Random House, Inc., 1745 Broadway, New York, NY 10019, and in Canada by
Random House of Canada Limited, Toronto. Random House and the Random House colophon are registered trademarks of Random House, Inc.

Library of Congress Control Number: 2009938766

ISBN: 978-0-375-85967-0

www.randomhouse.com/kids

MANUFACTURED IN CHINA

10 9 8 7 6

Joker and Two-Face were robbing the Gotham Bank. Suddenly, Joker pulled the alarm! *KLANG! KLANG! KLANG! KLANG! KLANG!*

"Are you crazy?" Two-Face growled. "Now Batman is going to come after us!"

"I can't help myself," Joker said, laughing. "I just love that sound!"

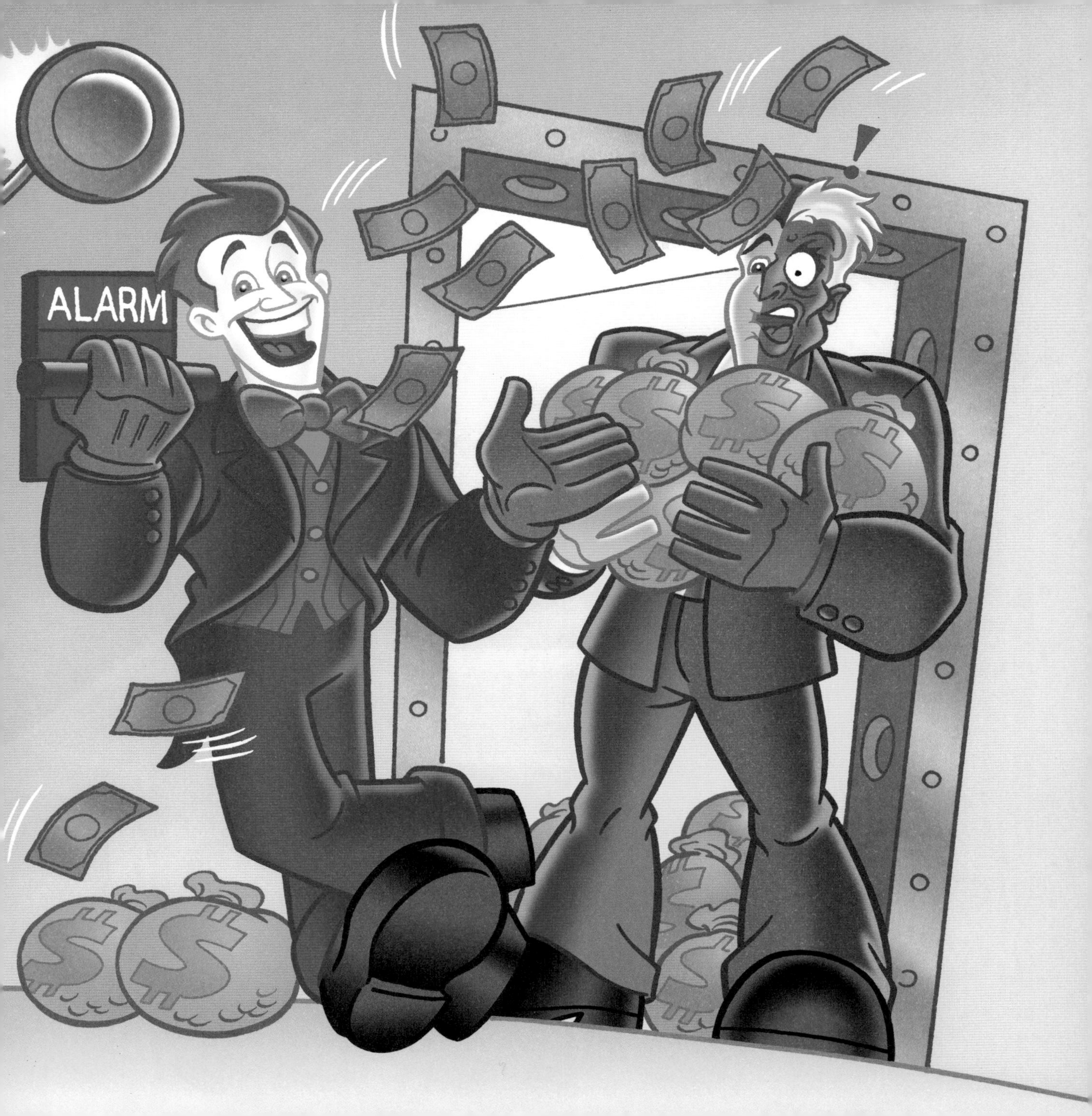
ALARM

Suddenly, Batman plunged through the bank's skylight!
He quickly lassoed Two-Face with the Batrope.
   "Since you're all tied up, I'll see you later!" Joker
shouted to Two-Face as he ran out the door.

Joker spotted the Batmobile parked in front of the bank. "Now, *that* is a getaway car!" he exclaimed. "Since Batman is busy with Two-Face, he won't mind if I take it for a spin."

The Batmobile's rocket-powered engines roared to life.
"Whoooooo-hoo!" Joker cried. He took off down the
streets of Gotham, holding on tight!

"Robin, meet me at the Gotham Bank with the Batcycle," Batman said into his communicator. "And call the Super Friends—Joker has the Batmobile!"

With Joker at the wheel, the Batmobile was out of control! He drove on sidewalks, knocked over street signs, and smashed into mailboxes.

"Let's see what this Batbuggy can really do," Joker said gleefully. He began flipping switches and pressing buttons, causing missiles to launch and flamethrowers to fire.

Luckily, the Super Friends arrived just in time. Superman and the Flash moved people to safety. Aquaman and Cyborg put the fires out, while Green Lantern and Hawkman stopped the missiles.

Batman and Robin caught up with Joker.
"Pull over, Joker!" Batman said. "This joyride is over."

"Sorry," Joker replied. "I don't brake for bats!"
Joker flipped another switch, releasing an oil
slick. Robin's ATV slid in the slippery mess!

"Whatever you do," Batman warned Joker, "don't pull the red lever under the seat."

"I love red levers as much as I love the sound of alarms!" Joker cried excitedly, pulling the lever. *KA-BOOF!* The Batmobile's ejector seat blasted Joker straight into the air!

Green Lantern scooped Joker out of the sky with a baby's car seat big enough to hold him tight.

"Is there a problem, Officers?" Joker asked the police sheepishly. "Was I speeding?"

"Your license is suspended—*permanently*," Batman said.

"What are you going to drive until the Batmobile is fixed?" the Flash asked Batman.

"The Jokermobile," Robin said, "has a full tank of gas."

"Maybe I'll just walk," Batman replied, and they all laughed.

. . . and the bad guys are on the run!

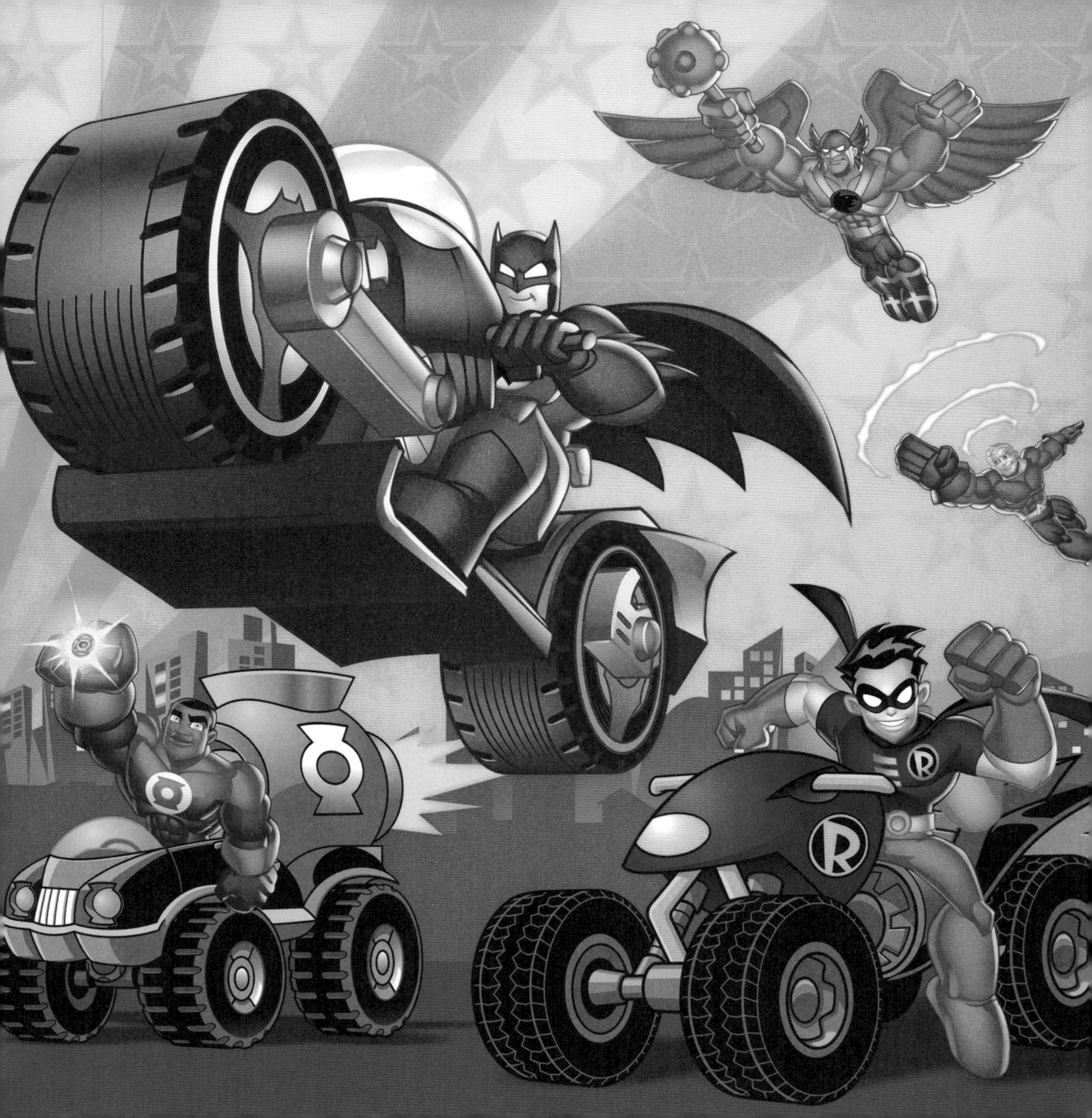

The Super Friends
are on the go . . .

Mr. Freeze's Ice Sled

Mounted with a subzero ice cannon, Mr. Freeze's Ice Sled can freeze anything in its path. Powerful tank treads keep Mr. Freeze moving so he can commit his frosty crimes.

Jokermobile

Armed with sprayers that spew metal-melting acid, and a deadly pie-launcher, the Jokermobile packs a punch. Joker thinks it's funny to use the Jokermobile to break the law, so be careful if this criminal contraption comes bouncing your way!

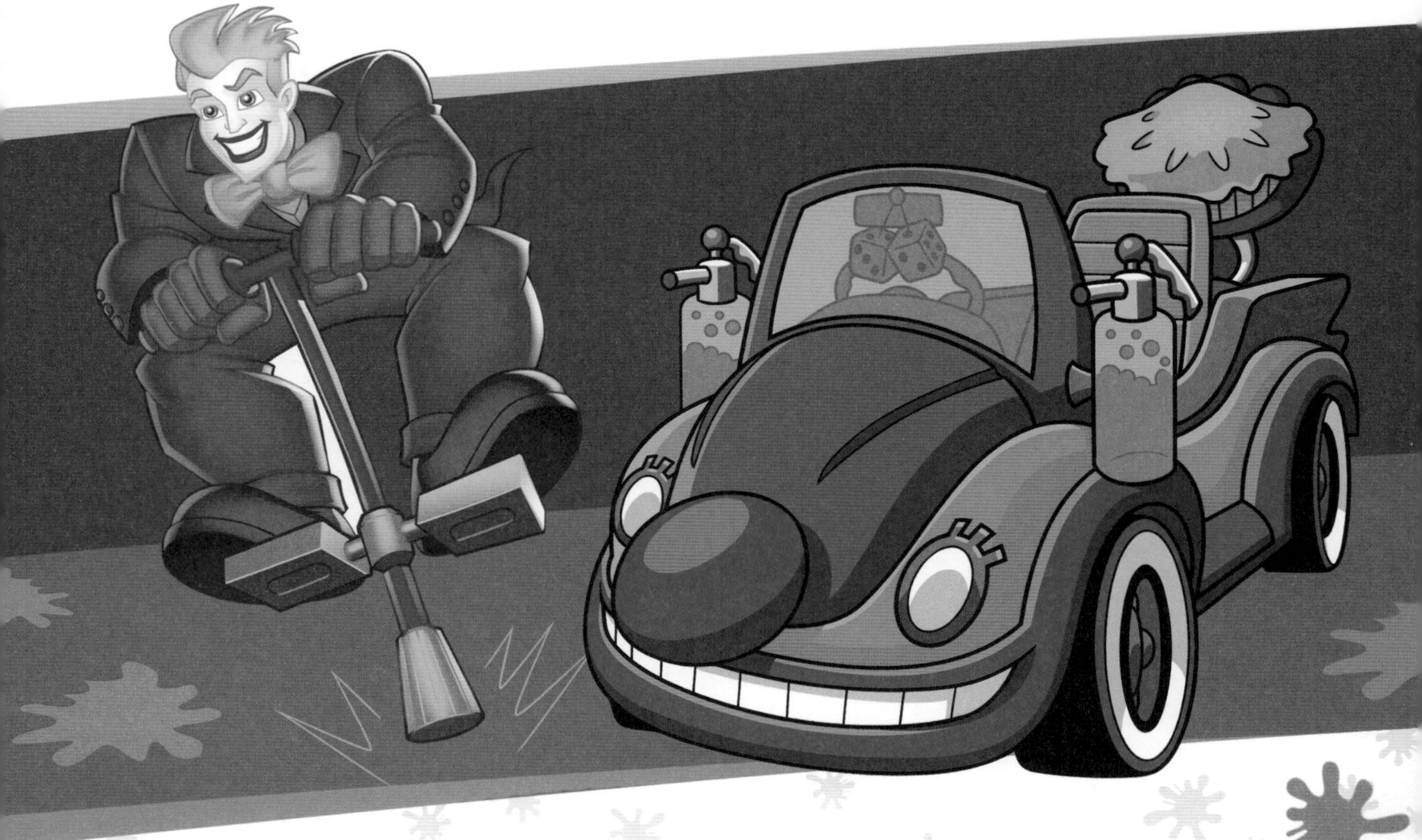

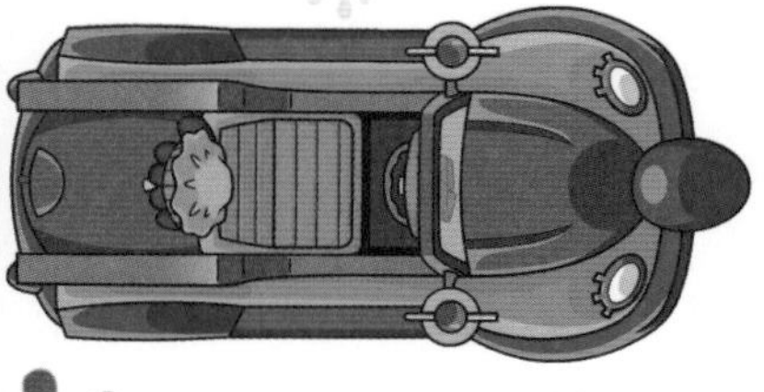

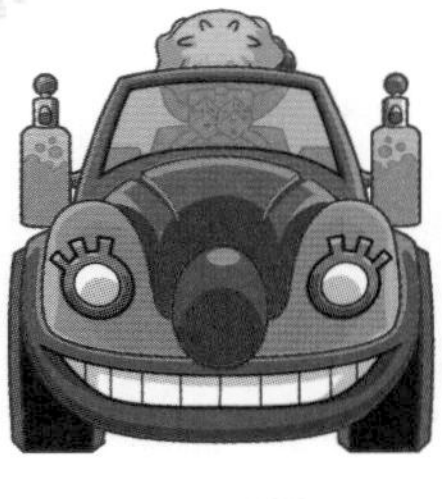

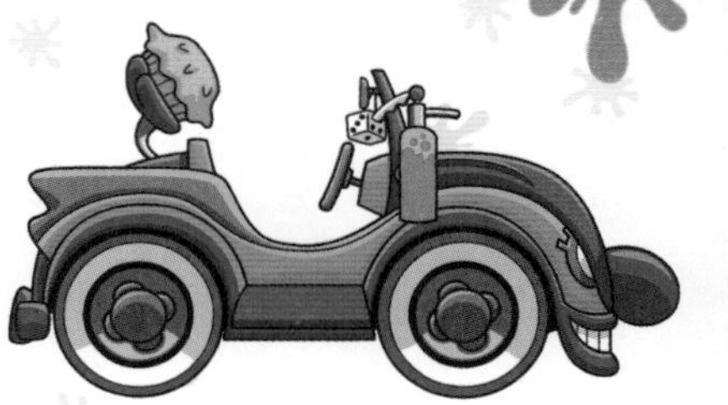

Aquaman's Aquasub

When Aquaman has to take the Super Friends to the very deepest parts of the ocean, he uses the Aquasub. This multipurpose submarine is perfect for undersea rescues and studying ocean life!

Green Lantern's Rocket Truck

Green Lantern's Rocket Truck is a rugged vehicle he uses to explore planets with harsh environments. Even molten lava and subzero ice are no match for this machine!

Robin's ATV

When Robin needs to go off-road, he takes his All-Terrain Vehicle. The ATV has the traction to climb mountains, bounce over boulders, and splash through mud. It can go anywhere the Boy Wonder needs to be to catch the bad guys!

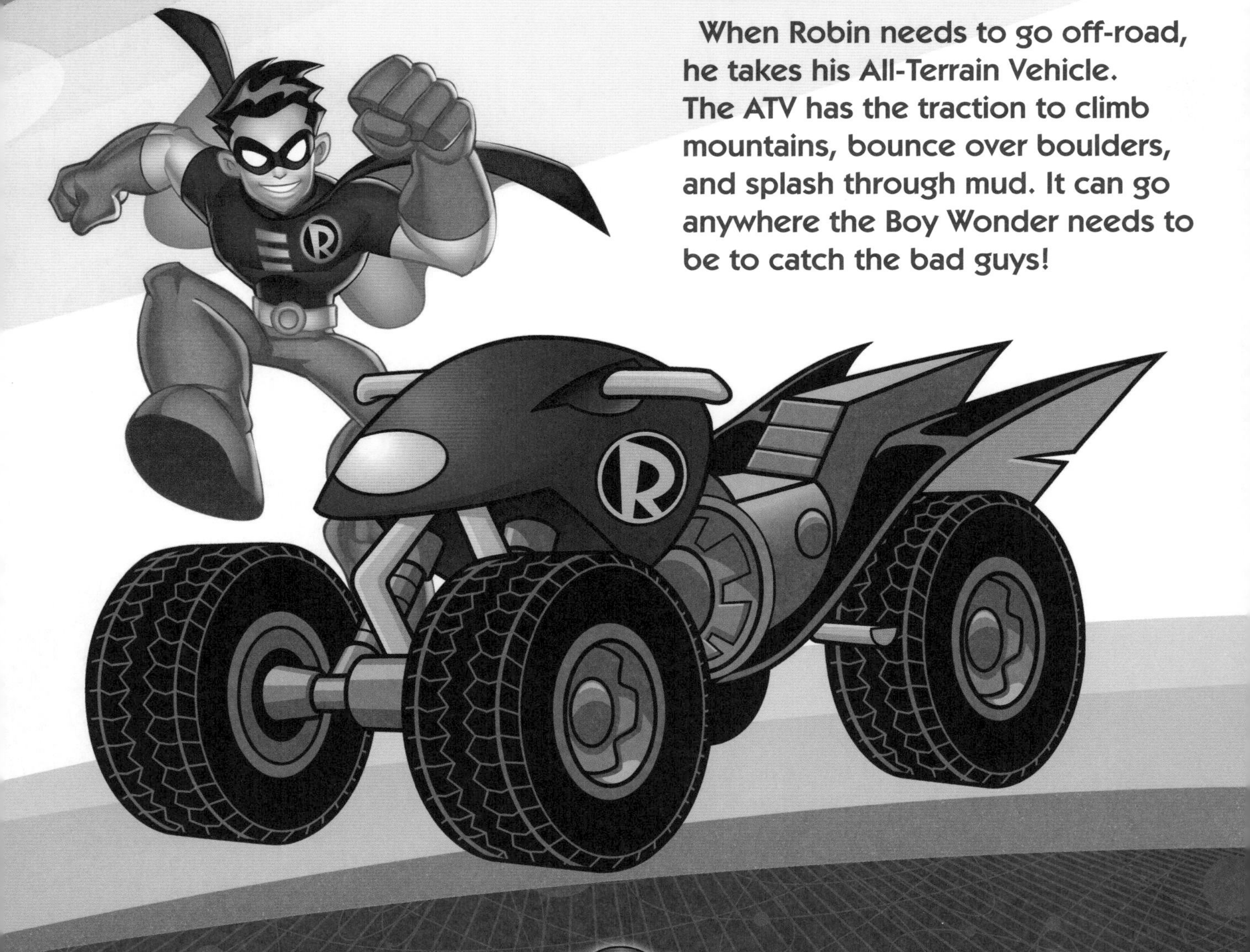

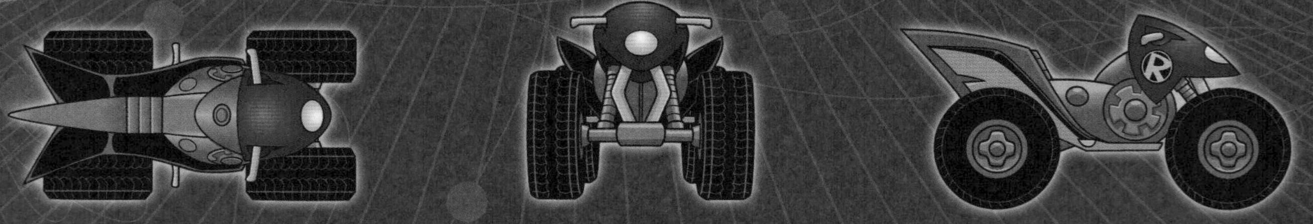

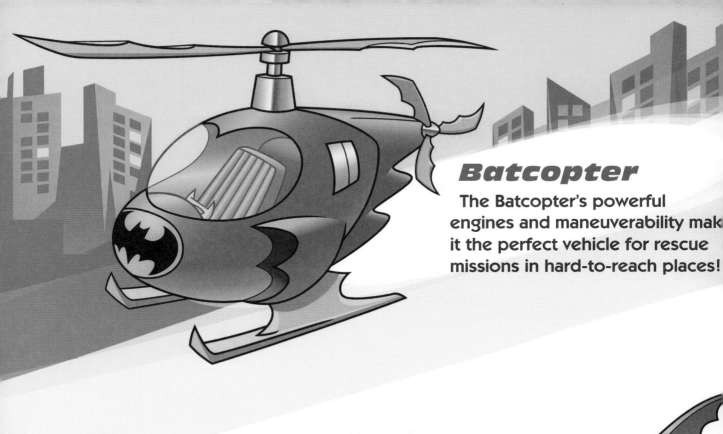

Batcopter

The Batcopter's powerful engines and maneuverability make it the perfect vehicle for rescue missions in hard-to-reach places!

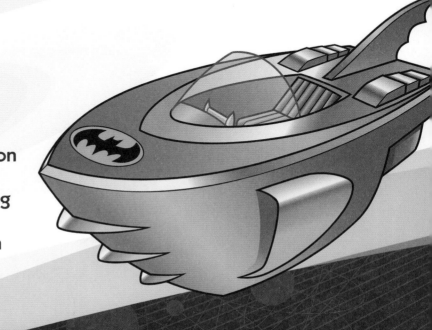

Batboat

Batman reels in the bad guys on the high seas with the Batboat! It's equipped with crime-fighting gear, including torpedoes and diving suits, just in case Batman and Robin's adventures take them underwater!

Batwing

When Batman needs to fly at the speed of sound, he takes off in the Batwing. Its supersonic jet engines are whisper-quiet, making it almost completely undetectable.

Batcycle

The two-wheeled Batcycle is
super-sleek, super-fast, and more
maneuverable than the Batmobile.

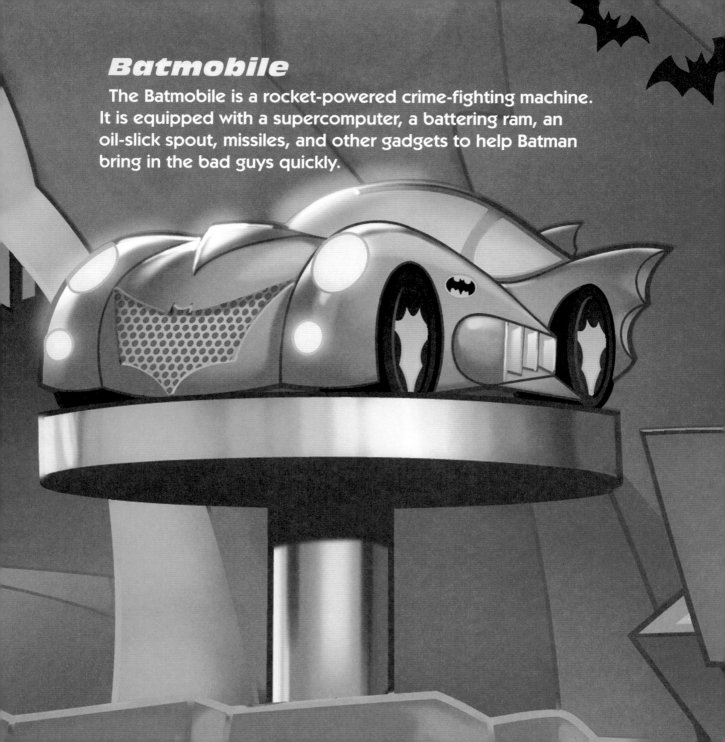

Batmobile

The Batmobile is a rocket-powered crime-fighting machine. It is equipped with a supercomputer, a battering ram, an oil-slick spout, missiles, and other gadgets to help Batman bring in the bad guys quickly.

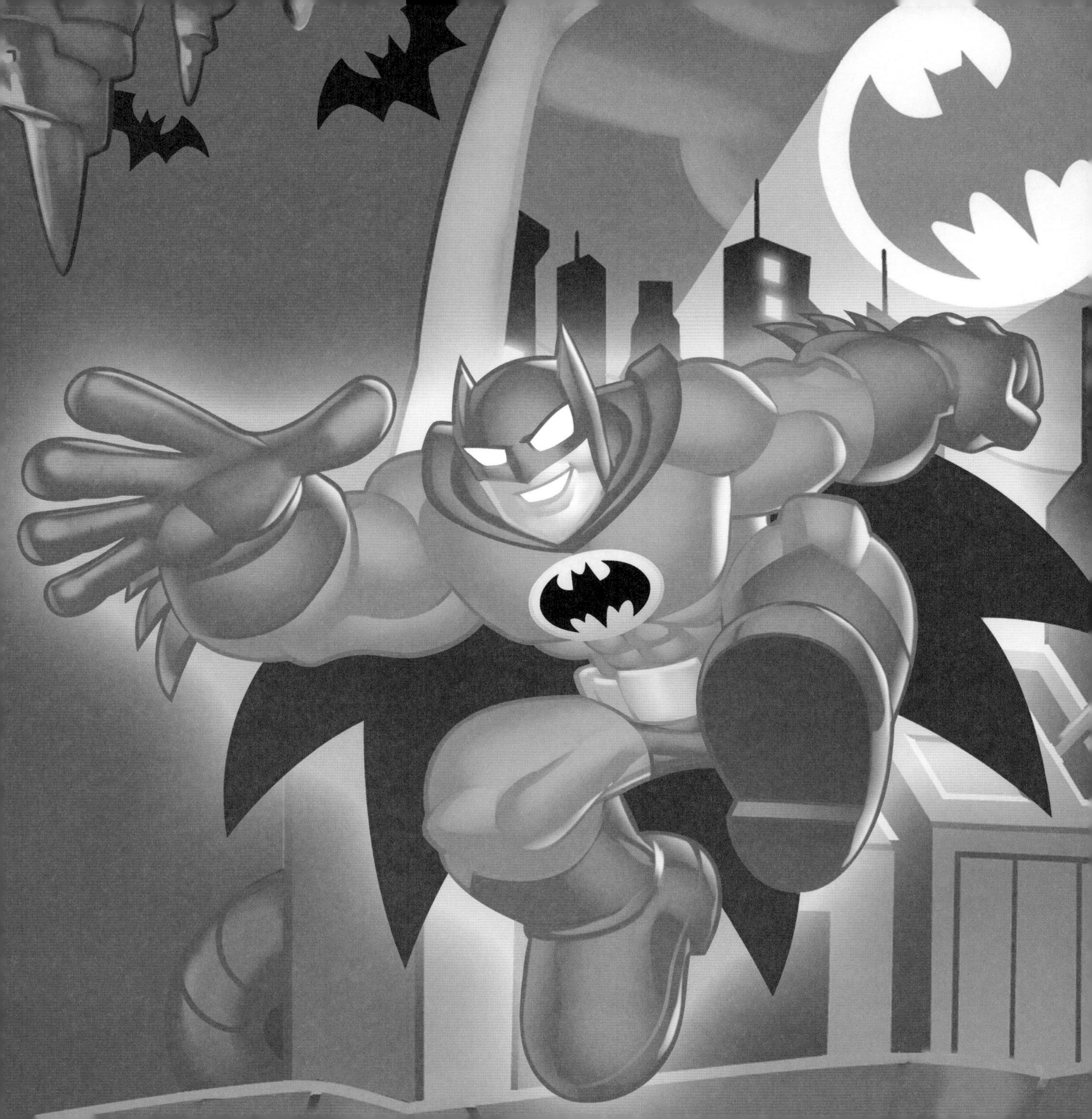

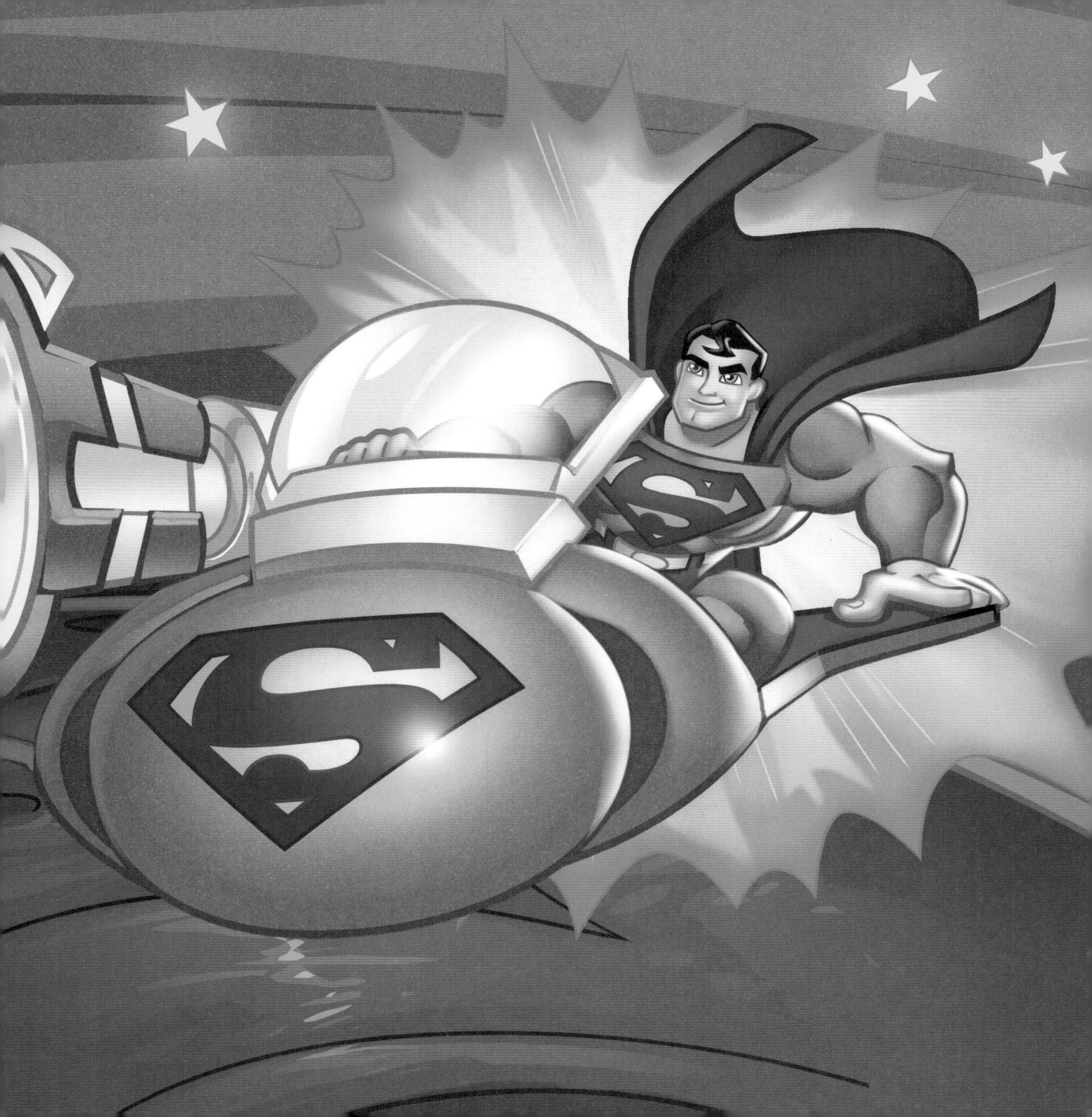

Superman's Space Sled

When Superman needs to handle kryptonite, the only substance in the universe that can harm him, he blasts off in his Space Sled. He uses the sled's mechanical claw to safely collect the kryptonite and keep it out of the hands of evildoers like Lex Luthor.

By D. R. Shealy

Random House 🏠 **New York**

DC SUPER FRIENDS and all related titles, characters, and elements are trademarks of DC Comics. Copyright © 2010 DC Comics. All rights reserved.
Published in the United States by Random House Children's Books, a division of Random House, Inc., 1745 Broadway, New York, NY 10019, and in Canada by
Random House of Canada Limited, Toronto. Random House and the Random House colophon are registered trademarks of Random House, Inc.

Library of Congress Control Number: 2009938766

ISBN: 978-0-375-85967-0

www.randomhouse.com/kids

MANUFACTURED IN CHINA

10   9   8   7   6